HE SCHOOL WAS deathly quiet and seemed to be deserted.

Nervously, I approached it from the road, followed a path round the side of the building and came to the main entrance. I tried the door but it was locked, so I rang the bell.

Footsteps approached. The door opened. A tall, pleasant-faced man with a grey moustache stood there.

"Good morning," I said. "I'm Miss Anderson. I have an appointment with the headmistress at ten o'clock."

"Oh, yes. Come in, Miss. I'm the caretaker." He stood aside for me to pass and closed the door again. "If you'll wait here, I'll see if Miss Leonard is ready for you."

He went along the corridor in front of me, turned to the right and vanished.

With my back to the front door, I looked round the hall. On the wall to my left was a green baize notice-board with a few notices neatly arranged and secured with drawing-pins. I wondered whether that board would still be so tidy when the vacation was over and the children were back. Past the notice-board were swing doors opening on to an empty gymnasium, its equipment idle, its floor shining with polish. The paintwork was fresh and the place looked as if it had just been redecorated. To my right were a number of other doors, closed and mysterious—for everything in an unfamiliar building seems mysterious. And ahead of me, to the left of the corridor and alongside it, was a flight of stairs leading upwards.

My nervousness increased. Interviews always panic me and I really needed this job. Trembling a little, I waited. The silence itself seemed to make a noise in my ears. I listened for the caretaker's returning footsteps.

Suddenly a woman appeared at the top of the stairs and began to descend. She startled me as she had made no sound in her approach, and I was reminded of one of my previous headmistresses whose habit of wearing soft-soled shoes had given her an uncanny ability to turn up silently when she was least expected. This woman on the stairs was pale, dark, very thin, and wearing a black dress unrelieved by any sort of ornament. Unsmiling, she looked at me with beautiful, but very unhappy dark eyes.

"Miss Leonard?" I said.

She didn't reply or even pause, merely moved towards the doors of the gymnasium. At the same moment I heard the caretaker's returning footsteps and turned to see him re-enter the corridor.

"This way, dear," he called. "Miss Leonard will see you now."

As I went towards him, I thought I smelt something burning, so hesitated. Again I looked through the glass at the top half of the gymnasium doors. The woman in black was out of sight.

"What's the matter?" The caretaker came up to me. "Feeling nervous?"

"Yes, I am—but it's not that—I thought I smelt burning."

He looked at me sharply. "No, not now," he said. "That's all over, and I should know.

But I've got a bonfire going in the grounds. Maybe the smoke is blowing this way."

"That'll be it. Anyway, I can't smell it anymore. Was that Miss Leonard I saw a second ago?"

"Where?" he asked.

"On the stairs, then she went into the gymnasium—"

"You're in a proper state of nerves, you are," he said, as I followed him along the corridor. "There's no one in the building today except you, me, and Miss Leonard, and she's in her office waiting for you. Coming on the staff, are you?"

"I hope so. I've applied for the job of English teacher."

"Good luck, then," he said.

We stopped outside a door.

"This is Miss Leonard's room, Miss." He knocked on the door. A voice called: "Come in!"

And I went into the headmistress's room.

Miss Leonard was at her desk, the window behind her. She rose immediately, a plump yet dignified figure with neat white hair and a pink suit which heightened the colour in her cheeks. She was utterly unlike the woman in black.

She smiled. "Do come right in and sit down, Miss Anderson. I'm glad to see you. It's not easy to find staff at a moment's notice at the end of the autumn term."

"It's not easy to find a job at this time either," I said. "Most schools are fixed up for the whole of the school year."

"We were too—then suddenly there was a vacancy. Now, you're twenty-five, you have a BA degree in English, and two years' teaching experience." She was looking at my letter of application which lay on her desk.

"That's right, Miss Leonard."

"You haven't been teaching for the past twelve months. May I ask why?"

"My mother and I went to live in Rome with my sister and her husband, who is Italian. Mother was ill and she wanted to see my sister again before—well, Mother's dead now so I decided to come back to England."

"And do you know anything about this school?"

"No. I simply answered your advertisement."

"I'm glad you did." She picked up a folder of papers and handed it to me. "In here I've enclosed your timetable for next term and detail of syllabus and set books. So you can 'do your homework' before you arrive."

"You mean I've got the job?"

"Yes. Why not?"

"That's marvellous. Thank you."

We talked for a while, then, as she took me back to the main door, she said: "You'll find the rest of the staff very nice and friendly."

"I think I've seen one of them already," I said.

"Really? Which one?"

"I don't know. It was just that she came down the stairs while I was waiting in the hall. She was wearing a black dress."

Miss Leonard said casually: "Staff do come back during the vacation sometimes, to collect forgotten property or whatever. Goodbye for the present, Miss Anderson. When you arrive on the first day of term, come to my office and I'll show you the staff room then take you to your first class."

And the interview was over.

Christmas passed, January began, diligently I studied my folder of information, and then, on the night before first day of term, snow fell. My lodgings were a train journey away from the school and on the very morning when I wanted to be punctual, my train stuck. Ice on the points. By the time I reached the school, I was late, and distraught.

Added to this, the school itself looked different under snow. I couldn't even find the path to the main door. I took a wrong path, lost myself wandering round the building, then peered through a classroom window.

Lights were on inside. About thirty-five little girls in white blouses and dark tunics were sitting at their desks and listening to the teacher. That teacher was the dark, thin woman in the black dress whom I had seen before. Fascinated, I stood and gazed. It was like watching a silent play, myself in the outside dark, the actors in the light, playing their parts.

In the front row of the class was a little girl with golden hair falling like bright rain over her shoulders. Next to her was a dark

child, her black hair cropped close as a boy's. And next to this one was a child with a mop of red curls.

All the pupils were attentive, but this red-haired child was gazing at the teacher with an expression of adoration. It was touching, yet a little alarming. No human being deserves that much young worship . . .

I retraced my steps along the wrong path in the snow, found the right one and finally reached the entrance door. It was not locked this time. I let myself in and hurried to Miss Leonard's room.

"Come in!" she called in answer to my knock.

As I went in I blurted out: "I'm so sorry I'm late. It was my train—the snow—"

"Never mind, Miss Anderson. I guessed as much. I'll take you to the staff room."

She led me up the stairs from the hall, along a first floor corridor, into a room. It was an ordinary staff room—notice board, lockers, cables, hard chairs, easy chairs, electric fire. The light was on but the room was empty—at least, I thought it was empty at first, then realized that someone was sitting in one of the chairs. I saw her only out of the corner of my eye, and she was in a chair in the far corner of the room, away from the fire; so although I recognized her as the woman in black, I didn't turn to look at her. If I thought anything, it was just that she had a bit of a nerve to leave her class, which I'd seen her teaching a few minutes ago, and come to sit in the staff room—and now she'd been caught out by the entrance of the headmistress.

Miss Leonard, however, took no notice of her. She said: "This will be your locker, Miss Anderson. The bell will ring any minute now for the end of first period, then I'll take you to your first class. It's a double period of English—you'll have seen that from your timetable. Mrs Gage is looking after them at the moment—she's our biology teacher—and she'll be glad to see you as by rights these first two periods should be her free ones. That's why the staff room is empty."

But the staff room was not empty. There was the woman in black, looking at me seriously, with those beautiful sad dark eyes . . .

Miss Leonard led the way to my first class. The teacher there looked quickly round as we entered. She was a lively, dark, fairly young woman with eagerly bent shoulders and black-rimmed spectacles. She wore a red sweater and brown skirt.

"Here we are, Mrs Gage," said Miss Leonard. "Now you'll get your second free period all right." She faced the class. "Now, girls, this is Miss Anderson, your new

English teacher. Help her as much as you can, won't you?"

And I too stood facing the class. It was the same class which I had seen through the window only fifteen minutes earlier. There was the child with fair hair in the front row, and the dark one next to her—and . . .

No. It was different. The child with curly red hair was not there.

Her desk was empty. And, of course, the teacher was different . . .

Miss Leonard and Mrs Gage left the room. I was on my own with this familiar, unfamiliar class. I spent the next forty minutes or so in trying to get to know them, checking on their set books, and so on, then the bell rang for morning break and I returned to the staff room.

The chair where the woman in black had been sitting was empty now but other chairs were occupied. The staff had gathered for elevenses. I heard someone say, above the noise of the many voices: "How does that damned chair get over into the corner like that? Who puts it there?"

"Night cleaners have strange ways," said another voice.

"Extraordinary about night cleaners," said the first. "They work here for years, and so do we—and which of us are the ghosts? We coexist, but never meet."

A woman in an overall came in with a tray bearing a pot of coffee and cups and saucers. Mrs Gage came over to me. "Coffee, Miss Anderson?"

"Oh—thank you."

"How do you like it?"

"Black. No sugar."

"Same here." She collected coffee for us both.

"Sorry you missed a free period because of me," I said. "My train got held up in the snow."

"That's all right."

Sipping my coffee, I studied the other women around me. "Doesn't everyone come here for coffee at break?" I asked Mrs Gage.

"Everyone! It's only our elevenses that keep us going."

"Then where is—well—one of the teachers? She was taking your class—my class—this morning—I saw her through the window—"

"Not that class," said Mrs Gage. "I started with them immediately after morning assembly."

"But it was that class. I recognized some of the girls. And the one with red hair wasn't there."

Mrs Gage looked at me sympathetically. "You're all upset over being late, aren't you? And maybe you're upset for other reasons too. I don't blame you. It's not easy to be taking Miss Carey's place."

"Miss Carey? Who—" But as I tried to ask more, the woman in the overall came to collect our dirty cups and the bell rang for third period. We all went off to our classes.

I still had one more period with the same class I'd taken before—or so I thought, until I reached the room. Then I saw that the teacher's chair was already occupied.

The woman in black sat there.

And the child with red hair was in the third desk in the front row.

"Sorry," I murmured, withdrew again, and stood in the corridor to re-examine my timetable. Surely I hadn't made a mistake— no—I was right—this was my class. So I went back. And the teacher's chair was empty now. So was the third desk in the front row...

That was when I began to be afraid. So afraid that a sick shiver travelled down my spine, sweat sprang out on my skin, and I needed all my self-control to face the class and give a lesson.

At the end of the lesson, when the bell rang for next period, I asked the class in general: "Where's the girl who sits there?" I indicated the third desk in the front row.

No one answered. The children became unnaturally quiet and stared at me.

"Well?" I said.

Then the fair-haired child said: "No one sits there, Miss." And the dark child next to her added: "That was Joan's desk."

"But where is Joan?" Silence again.

Then Mrs Gage walked in. "Hello, Miss Anderson. We seem to be playing Box and Cox this morning. Do you know which class to go to for last period?"

"Yes, thank you. I've got my timetable." I hurried away.

Busyness is the best panacea for fear, and I was very busy getting to know a different

class until the bell rang for lunch. Back to the staff room again—and it was full again—and there was Mrs Gage, kindly taking me under her wing.

"Miss Leonard asked me to look after you until you find your way around," she said. "The staff dining room is on the second floor. Would you like to come up with me?"

I was glad of the offer.

The staff, all female, sat at three long tables in the dining room, and the place was as noisy as a classroom before the teacher arrives! Two overalled women, one of whom I had seen at break, served our meal. Conversation was mostly "shop"—the besetting sin of female teachers. As the newcomer, I kept quiet, but I looked at those women one by one, trying to identify the woman in black.

She wasn't there.

Unhungry, I did my best with the meat pie and carrots, then when rice pudding and prunes arrived (for teachers have children's diet) I murmured to Mrs Gage: "Who is the member of staff who wears a black dress?"

She looked round. "No one, as far as I can see."

"No—she's not here—but I've seen her."

"Really? But I think everyone's here today. We do go out for lunch sometimes, but when the weather is like this it's easier to have it on the premises. What was she like?"

"Dark, pale, thin, not very young—with lovely eyes—"

"And wearing a black dress, you said?"

"Yes."

Mrs Gage gave a small, unamused laugh. "Sounds like Miss Carey, but you can't possibly have seen her."

"The one who's left—whose place I've taken—"

"No one could take Joanna's place."

"Oh—I didn't mean—"

"Miss Anderson, I'm sorry. I didn't mean anything either." She didn't look at me, but she had stopped eating her prunes.

"Did something bad happen to her?" I asked.

"She tried to burn down the school."

The words were whispered and the noise of voices around us was so loud that I thought I must have misheard, so I said: "What?"

"She tried to burn down the school," Mrs Gage repeated. Others at our table heard her this time. Conversation faded, ceased. Heads turned towards Mrs Gage.

"Don't all look at me like that," said Mrs Gage. "I'm only telling Miss Anderson what happened last term. She has a right to know." Leaving her sweet unfinished, she pushed back her chair with a scraping noise and left the room. I sat petrified. Murmurs of conversation began again, but no one spoke to me, so I pretended to eat a little more, then rose and left.

I found my way back to the staff room.

Mrs Gage, cigarette in hand, was sitting by the electric fire. "Sorry about that," she said. "Until you asked, I presumed you knew. It was in the newspapers."

"I've been living in Italy. I only came back just before Christmas. Could you tell me what happened, before the others return from lunch?"

"Sure. Have a fag. Rotten first day for you." She passed me a cigarette and lit it for me.

"This smell of burning," I said. "I've noticed it before."

"It's only our cigarettes, Miss Anderson. And we'd better get them smoked before the rest of the staff come back. Some of them abhor cigarette smoke. These spinsters!"

"I'm one too."

"Not really. You're still young. So you want to know about Joanna Carey?"

"Of course I do. After all, I've seen her. Did she get the sack, and now she comes back uninvited—or what?"

"My dear child, you can't have seen her. She's dead."

"Then whom did I see?"

Mrs Gage ignored this question. She said: "Miss Carey, Joanna, had been a teacher here for twenty years. She was excellent at her job and the kids adored her. Then, about a year ago, she changed."

"In what way?"

"Not in the way she taught. Her teaching was always brilliant. But in her attitude. After being most understanding and sympathetic with the young, she gradually became more and more cynical, to the point of cruelty. She made it clear to all of us, staff and pupils, that she now hated her job and only went on doing it because she had to earn a living somehow."

"But why did this happen?"

"Why? Who knows why anything? But in fact I do know more about her than most of the staff. Joanna and I were friends, before she changed. She often visited my husband and me, in the old days. She and I had occasional heart-to-hearts over the washing-up. So I learned something of her private life. She was the mistress of a married man, for about ten years. That *was* her private life. Then he ditched her—decided to 'be a good boy' again. When it happened, she told me, and she laughed, and didn't seem to care very much. But it was from that moment that she began to change, grow bitter, disillusioned. The world went stale for her. The salt had lost its savour. She began to take revenge, not against the man, but against everyone else with whom she came into contact. That meant us—staff and kids. She was filled with hate, and hate breeds hate. Even I, who had been her friend, began to avoid her. She was left alone."

"You said she tried to bum down the school."

"She did. She failed in that. But while she was trying, she burned herself to death. And one of the children."

"One of the children? Oh, no!"

"It's true, Miss Anderson. I wouldn't say it if it weren't. I, of all people, once so friendly with Joanna—I'd be the last person to admit it, if it weren't true. But it happened."

"What exactly did happen?"

"One Friday evening, towards the end of last term, she came back to school. This is what the police found out when they investigated afterwards. Everyone except Mr Brown, the caretaker, had gone. She soaked the base of the long curtains in the gymnasium with paraffin and set fire to them. Imagine the flare-up that would make—all those curtains in that big room. Why she didn't get away afterwards, no one knows. Maybe she fainted. Maybe she deliberately let herself be burned—like that Czech student—you know. People do these things. When they're desperate. Mr Brown saw the flames, sent for the fire service, and after they'd come and put out the fire, her body was found among the ashes of the curtains."

"And the child? You said—"

"Yes. Little Joan Hanley. A dear little girl with red curly hair. She adored Joanna. She was found there too, burned to death, among the ashes of the curtains."

"But how did she come to be there in the first place?"

"Once again, no one knows. She was one of Joanna's worshippers. There were several in the school. Girls' schools are diabolical in this respect. Rather like all-female wards in hospitals. Unnatural passions are aroused. Joan Hanley would have done anything in the world for Joanna Carey. So did Joanna invite the child to the 'party'? I don't know. But it looks like it."

"Didn't the police find out anything about why Joan Hanley was there?"

"They tried. She had told her parents that she was going to the cinema, which she often did on Friday nights. When she didn't come home at her usual time, her parents wondered—and the next thing they knew, the police were on their doorstep, telling them that their daughter had been burned to death at the school. That's all I know, Miss Anderson—all any of us knows. Since it happened, men have put the gymnasium to rights, hence all the fresh paint and the pretty new curtains. These tragedies are happening all the time, all over the world—

I know that—but when I think of Joanna, in her hatred and bitterness, drawing a child into such a burning—Oh God!" She put her hands over her face.

The staff room became deathly quiet. Only the two of us there, Mrs Gage and me, crouching over the electric fire, our cigarettes burning down, the silent snow covering the world outside—and God knows why I suddenly looked behind me.

I looked at that chair in the far corner of the room. It was no longer empty. The woman in black sat there. She looked straight at me, with those tragic eyes.

Then the staff room door burst open and the other women poured in, filling the quietness with noise, filling the empty chair with bodies, talking 'shop'—and I thought: No wonder Joanna Carey took a hate against all this. And yet—to burn a child—along with oneself—No!

"I didn't!" The sound came over, clearly, loudly, as if it filled the world. Yet no one seemed to hear it. It had spoken into my head only.

"I'll prove it," said the loud voice in my head. "Come!"

Mrs Gage was leaning back in the chair by the fire. She had lit another cigarette and closed her eyes. She looked tired out, and no wonder. I got up and left the room, that room full of talking women.

I walked, blindly yet guided, along the unfamiliar corridor. Outside, in the now, the children were having snowball battles. They were having a lovely lunch hour! Heaven was outside. Hell was within.

I walked, without knowing why, into the classroom which I had seen through the window, the classroom where I had taught during the second and third periods of the school morning.

I walked up to the third desk in the front row.

I sat down in that desk, as if I were the little girl, Joan Hanley, who had, day after day, sat down in that desk . . .

I opened the desk lid. There was nothing inside.

I looked at the scratchings and carved initials on the top of the desk lid.

I found: "J.H. LOVES J.C." And, over it, an unsymmetrical heart pierced by a rather wonky arrow.

But I knew already that J.H. had loved J.C. I had seen the child's face through the window, only this morning—I had seen what did not exist—yet which did exist—

What to do now?

My hand, guided, by God knows whom or what, put its fingers into the empty ink-well socket. The fingers found a closely folded piece of paper.

I unfolded it, carefully, and read:

"Dear Mum and Dad, I do not love you. I love Miss Carey. Where she goes, I go. I follow her everywhere. Tonight I have followed her to the school. She has gone to the gymnasium. I shall follow her there. Something is going to happen. That is why I am writing. Whatever she does, I shall do too. Because I love her. I must hurry now, to be with her. Funny really—as she does not even know I follow her! I'll put this under my inkwell. I don't expect you'll ever read it, but you never know. Yours sincerely—Your daughter, Joan."

"I didn't know she was there!" cried that voice in my head, loud with its silence. "I didn't know she was there!"

"Of course you didn't!" I answered aloud, loudly. "It's all right! I'll tell them!"

The classroom door opened and Miss Leonard walked in.

"Miss Anderson, what on earth are you doing?"

What on earth was I doing? I was sitting at a dead child's desk, a scrap of paper in my hand, and "talking to myself."

"I've found something, Miss Leonard." I passed her the letter. She read it. "So that's what happened," she said. "Miss Carey didn't take the child there with her at all. The little girl secretly imitated her goddess, even to the point of suicide. Where did you find the letter?"

"In the inkwell socket. I'm surprised it hasn't been found before, maybe by one of the children."

"No. I cleared that desk myself, removed the inkwell and didn't think to look underneath it. And the children never touch this desk. I did think of removing it, but that's too much like giving in to superstition. What made YOU look there, Miss Anderson?"

"She—she led me here—she spoke in my head—I don't understand it—but it happened—"

"You're psychic, aren't you? Did you know that already?"

"Not until I came to this school."

"You saw her on the day of your interview, didn't you?"

"Yes. On the stairs."

"I remember. And I fobbed you off with a practical explanation."

"Did you ever see her, Miss Leonard?"

"No. But Mr Brown did, more than once. And one of the children, last term, after the fire, insisted that Miss Carey wasn't dead as she'd seen her in the corridor. Neither of them was lying. Some individuals see and hear more than others. Have you been very frightened?"

"At first I wasn't, because I thought she was real. Later, I did feel frightened."

"And now?"

"Now I just feel desperately sorry for her. Her eyes, Miss Leonard. If you could have seen the sadness in her eyes!"

"Mr Brown mentioned that. You may talk to him if you like, but please no talk of ghosts with anyone else."

"Of course not. Anyway, I think she'll go away now. She'll be free of the place. She's been punished dreadfully. Maybe ghosts are people in purgatory and we see them around us all the time without realizing that they are ghosts."

"Maybe you do," said Miss Leonard, smiling a little.

The bell rang for the beginning of afternoon school. A wail of disappointment rose from outside. I looked out of the window, saw the children cease their snowballing and move obediently towards the building.

Only one figure moved away from the building, moved through the oncoming crowd of girls, who took no notice of her at all. She walked farther away, on and on, past the playground, across the snow-covered playing-field. A pale sun was shining and the snow dazzled, accentuating the thin, dark outline of the woman in black. She looked so utterly alone. Then a small figure began to follow her, running quickly and eagerly, and the sun turned the little figure's mop of red curls into a flame shaped like a rose.

The child overtook the woman in black and walked beside her, lightly, dancingly. And the two retreating figures cast no shadows on the snow, and left no footprints.

R osemary timperley (1920–1988) was a British author, screenwriter, and editor of ghost stories.

ETH'S COMICS AND drawings have
appeared in the *New York Times*, the
New Yorker, the *Globe and Mail*, and
countless other publications.

His graphic novel *Clyde Fans* won the presti-
gious Festival d'Angoulême's Prix Spécial du Jury.

He lives in Guelph, Ontario, with his wife,
Tania, in an old house he has named "Inkwell's
End."

Library and Archives Canada Cataloguing in Publication

Title: The mistress in black : a ghost story for Christmas /
Rosemary Timperley ; designed & decorated by Seth.
Names: Timperley, Rosemary, 1920–1988,
author | Seth, 1962– illustrator.
Description: Series statement: Seth's Christmas ghost stories
Identifiers: Canadiana 20250253151
ISBN 9781771966726 (softcover)
Subjects: LCGFT: Ghost stories. | LCGFT: Short stories.
Classification: LCC PR6070.I4 M57 2025 | DDC 823/.914—dc23

Readied for the press by Daniel Wells
Illustrated and designed by Seth
Copyedited by Ashley Van Elswyk
Typeset by Ingrid Paulson

PRINTED AND BOUND IN CANADA